The fluppets® Storybook

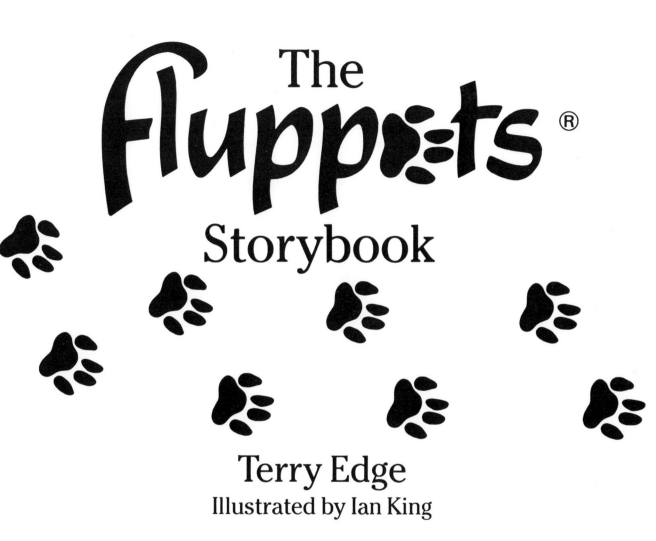

Terry Edge
Illustrated by Ian King

Hutchinson

London · Melbourne · Auckland · Johannesburg

First published in Great Britain in 1987
by Hutchinson Children's Books
An imprint of Century Hutchinson Ltd
Brookmount House, 62-65 Chandos Place,
Covent Garden, London WC2N 4NW

Century Hutchinson Australia (Pty) Ltd
16-22 Church Street, Hawthorn, Melbourne,
Victoria 3122

Century Hutchinson New Zealand Limited
32-34 View Road, PO Box 40-086, Glenfield,
Auckland 10

Century Hutchinson South Africa (Pty) Ltd
PO Box 337, Bergvlei 2012, South Africa

Designed by ACE Limited

Set in ITC Cheltenham Book by
Rowland Phototypesetting (London) Ltd

Printed and bound in Portugal
by Printer Portuguesa

British Library Cataloguing in Publication Data
Edge, Terry
  The Fluppet storybook.
  1. Title 2. King Ian
  823′.914[J]   PZ7

ISBN 0-09-172729-4

 # Felicity and Totty McScottie

Early one morning Felicity returned to her earth after spending the night hunting for food on the other side of Woad Wood. She was tired and ready to sleep, but just as she was about to duck into the main entrance, she heard a horrible noise from inside. 'Zorr – Korr Zorr – Korrrrr!'

'Somebody's snoring in my earth!' she said. 'I'd better find out who it is!'

Hiding behind a tree, she let out a long, loud howl. Suddenly, the snoring stopped and a little dog appeared. 'Who is there?' it said, sleepily.

'Felicity,' said Felicity. 'I'm a fox. And you're in my home.'

'I'm Totty McScottie,' replied the dog. 'I've run away from the dirty old town to live a natural life in the wood.'

Felicity laughed. 'The natural life isn't that easy you know. You'll soon see. Now, excuse me but I'm going to sleep.'

When night-time came again, Felicity woke up to find Totty McScottie yawning outside. 'I've been playing today,' he said, 'chasing my tail and jumping in streams – that sort of thing. But now I'm starving! Where's my dinner?'

'Over the river and down by the sea,' said Felicity. 'If you follow me, you might catch something.'

'Catch?' said Totty. 'Do cans of food have legs in the woods?'

'No,' replied Felicity, 'but crabs do.'

Down at the sea shore, Felicity found lots of little things to eat. But Totty just splashed about in the rock pools. He did chase one large crab but it pinched him on the end of his nose and, by the time he'd shaken it off, he was so tired he fell fast asleep on the sand.

Just before dawn, Felicity woke him up. 'It's time to go home,' she said.

'Where's my breakfast?' complained Totty.

'Under the water by now,' replied Felicity. 'The tide came in while you were asleep.'

'But I'm hungry!'

Felicity laughed. 'You had your chance. In Woad Wood, we don't play with our food – we eat it!'

The next night they found little to eat on the sea shore.

'We'll have to take some fish from the fisherman's hut,' said Felicity.

'But it doesn't belong to us!' cried Totty.

'We foxes have a saying,' replied Felicity. '"Food belongs to the hungry."'

Inside the hut Totty soon forgot his words and jumped eagerly into a box of shiny mackerel. But after only a few minutes he jumped out. 'Right,' he said. 'I've finished now. Let's go.'

'We have to eat as much as we can', said Felicity, 'whether we want to or not. The cold weather's coming soon and food will be short. You need to put weight on now.'

'No need,' said Totty, trotting out of the hut. 'There'll be more food tomorrow.'

Totty played all night and he was just about to nod off the next morning when he noticed Felicity busily digging. 'What on earth are you doing?' he asked in amazement.

'Storing food for the winter,' said Felicity, as she buried a fish in the hole.

'What a waste of time!' retorted Totty.

'Suit yourself,' replied Felicity. 'But you won't find much food in the winter in Woad Wood!'

Cold rain poured into Woad Wood right through the day and when Felicity and Totty woke up there were huge puddles everywhere.

'We won't reach the sea tonight,' said Felicity. 'The river will be too deep for us to cross.'

'What will we eat, then?' moaned Totty.

'My friend Bumper's favourite food!' laughed Felicity, bounding off into the rain.

Totty quickly followed, catching up with Felicity in the middle of a soggy clearing. 'There's nothing here,' said Totty, 'except worms.'

'Worms it is!' said Felicity. 'Dig in!'

'Ugh!' said Totty. 'All right for you, perhaps; but much too slimy for me.'

After another night with no food, Totty woke up feeling very hungry indeed. 'Are we going out?' he asked, rushing outside. 'I haven't eaten in days!'

But everything looked different; the ground was covered in heaps of thick white snow, and he couldn't even find his way to the sea.

Felicity eventually decided that she would go in search of food, despite the cold.

'But how will you find your way?' asked Totty.

'Didn't you memorize the shapes of the trees and bushes when you had plenty of time to, in the summer?' said Felicity.

'I was playing!' protested Totty.

'So was I,' said Felicity. 'But not all the time.'

Totty followed her to the sea and watched miserably as Felicity dug up the fish she'd buried in the good weather. 'Can I have some?' he asked.

Felicity smiled. 'If you want to live in the woods, you'll have to feed yourself. But I tell you what: you can have any fish that you can find without my help!'

Totty scampered about the snowy shore digging holes everywhere; but he couldn't find any fish.

'Use your nose!' shouted Felicity.

'I can dig better with my paws!' replied Totty.

'I mean use your nose to *smell* the fish with,' said Felicity.

Totty tried, but found that his nose was so cold he couldn't smell anything at all. His stomach was aching with hunger now. 'I'm going back to town,' he declared.

'Are you sure you won't wait till spring?' said Felicity. 'There's plenty to eat then.'

'Maybe so,' replied Totty. 'But in the meantime I'd have to make do with snow and frozen worms. Ugh!'

'Goodbye then.'

'Goodbye Felicity. Er . . . . how do I get home from here?'

Felicity laughed. 'Just follow the sea until you come to the harbour, then turn right.'

On her way home, Felicity met Bumper. 'What's happened to Totty McScottie?' he asked.

'Gone back to town,' replied Felicity. 'He was hungry.'

Bumper laughed. 'Everyone in Woad Wood is hungry at this time of year.'

'But he's used to having his dinner brought to him every day, rain or shine.'

'He's probably better off in town then,' replied Bumper.

'Yes,' said Felicity. And then she looked thoughtful. 'He was rather silly sometimes. But do you know something – I think I'm going to miss him!'

And the two friends disappeared into the trees of Woad Wood.

Inside Woad Wood, Renée was amazed to discover that everywhere she looked there was long, luscious grass. She hopped further and further from home, nibbling away happily.

But just as night was falling, she jumped around a tree and came face-to-face with a pair of black, shiny eyes surrounded by hard, spiky fur. 'An enemy!' she gasped.

'Not an enemy,' said the hedgehog, 'an *'Enery*. Henry H. Hogg, to be precise.'

'Will you eat me?' asked Renée.

'I might, if you were twelve sizes smaller and didn't hop about so much,' laughed Henry. 'Slugs are more my size *and* they don't jump very far.'

'I'm brave and strong!' said Renée. 'But I'm lost and feeling tired, too. Do you know where I can sleep?'

'There's a place just over there,' said Henry. 'I don't think anyone lives in it any more.'

'Thanks, Mr Hogg,' said Renée, running straight for the cobweb-covered tunnel entrance.

The tunnel was much longer and wider than a rabbit's warren and Renée began to wonder what kind of creature could have made such a big house. Carefully, she crept into a large side room, full of dry, musty grass.

There was an old, peculiar smell in the air that made her whiskers twitch in fear but she was so tired that she soon curled up and fell asleep on the grass.

A booming noise woke her. A set of very big feet were pounding down the tunnel! 'Ah-hah!' said a voice. 'What's this my old snout detects? It's certainly not a worm! Much bigger and tastier, I should say.'

Renée burrowed deeper into the grass.

'I do believe,' the voice grew closer, 'it's a rabbit!'

Renée peeped through the grass and screamed at the biggest, most fearsome face she'd ever seen!

'I'm glad I decided to patrol this old set tonight,' said the badger. 'I haven't eaten rabbit for a long time!'

'I'm strong!' squeaked Renée.

'So are my teeth!' replied the badger.

Renée took a deep breath, hopped straight over his head and fled up the tunnel. It wasn't until she was a safe distance from the set that she risked a glance behind her. The badger was nowhere to be seen. 'I was too fast for him!' she shouted. 'He couldn't catch me!'

She hopped on through the trees until she came to an emerald clearing, sparkling with dewy grass. 'Breakfast,' sang Renée, '*and* dinner *and* tea!'

But just as she was swallowing her first mouthful, she saw a big red shape appear at the other side of the clearing.

A fox!

Renée was sure the fox was an enemy yet, as she watched, it began to dance! Surely enemies don't dance, she thought.

All around the clearing, the fox jumped and rolled and even tried to catch the clouds! Renée sat with her mouth open, staring at the wonderful show.

She didn't notice that the fox was gradually dancing closer.

Suddenly it pounced on her, holding her down with its powerful paws and closing its enormous mouth around her neck!

'Maybe I'm not so brave and strong after all, and I'm certainly not safe now!' cried Renée, waiting to be eaten.

'It's just that you're too young to understand the ways of the wood,' said the fox, who had let Renée go.

'What's your name?' whispered Renée.

'I'm Felicity. You're lucky; I'm a friendly fox, and one who isn't particularly hungry at the moment.'

'But I beat the badger!' said Renée.

Felicity laughed. 'That was only Bert Bentknees. He's too old to catch his own tail – let alone a rabbit. Come on, I'll take you home.'

Felicity led Renée through the wood towards Woad Warren. 'To be safe you don't only need to be brave and strong,' said Felicity, 'you must be clever too.'

'What do you mean?' asked Renée.

'Do you remember the game you played with Uncle Toughtoes?' said Felicity. 'It wasn't just a game, you know: every time your uncle thumped the ground you can be sure an enemy wasn't very far away.'

'Gosh, that *is* clever.'

'Here you are – home again!' said Felicity. 'I'd better disappear before Uncle Toughtoes sees me.'

Renée was worried that her family would be angry with her for running away. But she found that everyone was delighted to see her. And they all cheered when she told them about the new feeding places she'd found in Woad Wood.

'Well done,' said Mum. 'Every warren needs a rabbit who will go out alone and start a new warren when the old one becomes too crowded. With all the lessons you've learned, you'll have no trouble finding us a new home when the spring comes. You're very brave and strong.'

'And *clever*,' added Renée, remembering the most important lesson of all.

Henry and
the hibernation Hog-Many

Henry H. Hogg was hungry but he couldn't find a single crunchy beetle or crispy earwig to eat. 'Where do they all disappear to at this time of year?' he grumbled to himself. Then he bumped into something cold and twitchy in the long grass.

'Ah!' he said. 'I've found a slug. Good old slugs – they never let you down!' And he took a bite.

'Owww!' yelled Furze E. Pig, Henry's friend. 'Leave my snout alone!'

'Bless my spines!' said Henry. 'I thought your snout was a slug!'

'Does it look like one?' said Furze crossly. 'Anyway Henry, you shouldn't still be eating. It's Hog-Many tonight, and after that all us hedgehogs must hibernate for the winter.'

'I'm not,' grumbled Henry. 'It's a waste of time.'

'But if you don't, you'll starve,' said Furze. 'There isn't enough food for everyone when it's cold.'

'*I'll* find some,' said Henry, running off into Woad Wood.

Soon, Henry was in a dark part of the wood that he didn't know very well. He still couldn't find anything to eat and was just about to turn for home when he suddenly fell down a hole in a bank.

'Good of you to drop in, Mr Hogg,' said a voice. 'But why aren't you at the Hog-Many?'

'Who is there?' gulped Henry, peering into the darkness at the bottom of the hole. All he could see was a pair of huge eyes, moving towards him. And then he recognized a familiar smell.

'Felicity Fox! Thank goodness it's you!'

'I'm not going to the Hog-Many,' said Henry as Felicity pushed him up the steep slope of the tunnel.

'You'll upset everything in Woad Wood if you don't,' replied the fox. 'We foxes can't hibernate, so when it's cold we have to eat the worms and insects which you normally eat.'

'Oh, I see,' said Henry, feeling foolish.

'Look,' said Felicity, 'I've heard that in the garden at the edge of the wood there are hundreds of slugs just lying around on the earth – even in winter.'

'Thanks, Felicity,' smiled Henry. 'I'm off!'

To keep his mind off his empty tummy, Henry sang his favourite two lines of the Hedgehog Hunting Song –

'Slugs are juicy; slugs make you glow;
What's even better; slugs are slow!'

He sang all the way to the edge of Woad Wood, until his snout suddenly bumped into a high garden fence.

'Found it!' he shouted, ducking under the fence and into the garden. 'Hmmm, plenty of hedgehog-prints here. I didn't realize any of us came out this way.'

'Your lot don't, as a rule,' said a voice behind him.

Henry jumped. 'Who's that?'

'Spike T. Spokes at your service, squire.'

'Bless my spines!' said Henry. 'You're big for a hedgehog!'

Spike yawned. 'Well there's tons of grub round here you see,'

'Slugs?' asked Henry excitedly.

'Millions – if you like that sort of thing,' replied Spike. 'Personally I prefer variety myself, especially with the occasional drop of bread and milk to liven things up.'

'What's bread and milk?'

'Really, you wood hogs aren't very clever, are you?' said Spike, yawning again. 'But I can't be bothered to explain now; I'm going inside the house.'

'What's a house?' asked Henry.

But Spike didn't hear him. He was already waddling off towards a large square of light at the end of the garden.

Strange hedgehog, thought Henry; and then he suddenly caught sight of two big black slugs sparkling on the lawn. 'Ah, supper!'

Henry treated himself to a wonderful supper of slugs. Then he thought about inviting all his friends from Woad Wood to the feast. But 'No, why should I?' he decided. 'All the more for me.'

Just as he was smiling at his good luck, he began to feel very ill. His insides were burning, his head was dizzy and he felt sick. With a very great effort he pulled himself into the shelter of a nearby paper bag.

And then he passed out.

When he woke up later to find the whole world swaying from side to side, he thought he was going to die. But then the swaying stopped.

With a struggle, he poked his nose out of the bag. There was Felicity, just as if she had known he was going to be ill.

'I thought you'd get into trouble,' she said, 'so I followed you. I carried your bag in my teeth.'

'Oh . . .,' groaned Henry, 'why do I feel so ill?'

'The slugs must have been poisoned,' said Felicity.

'Why should anyone do that?' asked Henry, amazed.

'I've heard the owners of the garden don't like slugs,' replied Felicity. 'Slugs eat their vegetables. Come on, Henry, back in your bag and I'll take you to the Hog-Many. I've already told them to expect you.'

When they'd reached the edge of a clearing in Woad Wood, Felicity dropped the bag and Henry crawled out.

'Happy Hog-Many; see you in the spring, Henry!' called Felicity as she trotted into the wood.

Henry looked through the trees. It was a magical sight. There were hundreds of hedgehogs in a large circle and they were all dancing.

'We've been waiting for you, Henry,' said Furze E. Pig, making a space for him. Henry began to feel better.

After the dance everyone said goodbye for the winter and went off to their winter nests.

'I didn't bother to build a nest, Furze,' said Henry feeling rather silly.

Furze laughed. 'Follow me, Henry. You'll soon cheer up when you see this.'

He led Henry to the bottom of an old oak tree and showed him a tidy little mound of leaves and twigs hidden in its trunk. 'We all helped to build it,' said Furze. 'We knew you'd come.'

'Thanks, Furze,' said Henry.

Furze yawned. 'Good night, Henry.'

'Good *winter*, you mean,' said Henry. And then he went into his nest, curled into a ball and fell fast asleep.

Bumper and the invisible monsters

It was dark in Woad Wood and time for Bumper to be up and about. But he was feeling sorry for himself. Tomorrow was Cubs' Night, when all the young badgers would announce their new names, and Bumper would be the only cub without one.

His brother, Basher, was going to call himself Basher Strongpaws because he was so good at digging. His cousin, Arthur, was going to call himself Arthur Swiftpaws because he was so good at running. But Bumper wasn't good at anything. He couldn't even smell very well.

Because Badgers only come out in the dark, they don't use their eyes very much. Instead , they tell where they're going by sniffing. But only last week Bumper had been out hunting for wild honey when an angry bee had stung him with a direct hit on the tip of his snout. He hadn't been able to smell anything since.

'Oh, dung beetles!' Bumper said to himself. 'I'm hungry, so I suppose I'll have to get up now. He walked slowly up the long tunnels of the family set until he came to the entrance. 'Now, let's see what's going on in Woad Wood tonight,' he said. 'Doesn't seem to be anybody around—'

Suddenly he was interrupted. BASH! His brother Basher had jumped on his head! Together they tumbled down the slope and crashed into the old fallen log at the bottom.

'Ha!' shouted Basher. 'You didn't see me again. No-Nose!'

'Big-Smeller!' replied Bumper, jumping at his brother. And then the chase was really on!

Round and round the old trunk they dashed, then up the slope and down again.

Dad was watching. 'Now, stop it you two', he said. 'Why don't you make yourselves useful for a change and go and find some worms?'

'But Dad,' said Basher, 'there aren't any worms left in Woad Wood. They've all been eaten. We'll have to cross the Long Black Track to the meadow if we want some more.'

'Don't you dare!' shouted Mum. 'The Invisible Monsters that fly down it will squash you flat!'

The two brothers trotted away from their set and deep into Woad Wood.

'What can you smell, Bash?' asked Bumper.

Basher stopped and sniffed at the path. 'Here's where a stoat ran across, three days back. And here, if I'm not mistaken, is where Felicity Fox stopped to scratch herself only a few minutes ago!'

'You are clever,' said Bumper.

Basher placed a friendly paw on his shoulder. 'Never mind, Bump. Perhaps you'll be good at finding worms and then you can call yourself Bumper Wormfinder.'

But they had no luck finding their favourite food. Eventually, Basher said he was going home, to make sure he had plenty of sleep before Cubs' Night.

When he was alone, Bumper had a terrible but exciting idea. 'I'll go to the Long Black Track by myself and find a way across!' And without thinking further he ran off, deeper into the trees.

Just as he was pushing his way into the bushes at the edge of the road, he felt a powerful rumbling under his paws. 'It must be an Invisible Monster!' he gulped.

He was terrified. Slowly he poked his head through a gap in the leaves – there was a great flash of light and a thunderous roar!

aaarrRROOOMMMMMMM! A car shot by.

Bumper covered his ears with his paws and trembled.

And then – aarrRROOOMMMM! Another car!

'Going the other way this time!' he shouted. 'How ever will I cross the Long Black Track with so many Monsters about?'

'Why don't you do what I do?' said a strangely familiar voice. Bumper's weak eyes could just make out a smudge of red fur, bobbing across the road towards him.

'Felicity!' he cried.

Felicity slipped into the hedge beside him. 'We foxes are never squashed,' she said.

'But how can you tell if the Monsters are coming when they don't have any smell?' asked Bumper.

'I'll give you a clue,' she smiled. 'Whiskers!' And then, in a flash, she was gone.

Bumper watched the road.

aaarrRROOOMMMMM!

'Whiskers,' he said to himself.

All the badgers in Woad Wood had forgotten what their whiskers were for. Old Uncle Greatgob said he used his for picking his teeth, but nobody believed him.

aaarrRRROOOMMMM!

Bumper concentrated hard on his whiskers. And then, gently at first, he felt the tips of them shaking. I wonder . . . . he thought.

Then his whiskers twitched harder, began to jerk and –

aarrRROOOMMMM!

As the roar of the car had faded away, Bumper was amazed to find his whiskers had now stopped twitching. Carefully, he crept down to the edge of the road. His whiskers trembled again and he scampered back. He was just in time.

aarrRROOOMMMM! Another car shot by.

Ah, now he understood. When his whiskers shook it meant a Monster was coming. And when his whiskers were still it was safe. He took a deep breath, yes his whiskers were still. He squeezed his eyes tightly together and rushed straight across.

Suddenly he was safe in the meadow! Bumper looked around him and noticed something new – lots of shiny red round things lying on the grass. They looked good to eat. He picked one up and bit into it: it was delicious!

Bumper's mouth began to water, but he stopped himself from tucking in. 'I must fetch everyone else first,' he said.

Using his whiskers, he ran back over the road and through Woad Wood, all the way home. 'Come on, follow me!' he shouted. 'Something new for tea.'

Mum, Dad and Basher followed him to the road. When they saw him running to and fro across it, they thought he'd gone mad. 'Come back at once!' said Mum.

'It's all right,' yelled Bumper. 'I've learned to use my whiskers!' Soon he'd led them safely across to the meadow and everyone was tucking in to the juicy red apples.

Next night, at Cubs' Night, Bumper was proud to step forward in front of everybody.

'Now, what's your new name, Bumper?' asked Old Uncle Greatgob, who was Cub Leader.

'Bumper Wisewhiskers!' said Bumper.

And it was.